Robert Quackenbush

Texas Trail
to Calamity

A Miss Mallard Mystery

•

Prentice-Hall Books for Young Readers

A Division of Simon & Schuster, Inc.
New York

Prentice-Hall Books for Young Readers is a
trademark of Simon & Schuster, Inc.
Printed in Spain

Library of Congress Cataloging-in-Publication Data

Quackenbush, Robert M.
    Texas trail to calamity.

    Summary: When her horse runs away with her across
the desert, Miss Mallard, the famous ducktective,
finds herself at a forbidding ranch where she must
spend the night despite mysterious warnings about
her safety.
    [1. Mystery and detective stories.   2. Ducks—
Fiction.   3. West (U.S.)—Fiction]   I. Title.
PZ7.Q16Te   1986   [Fic.]   86-4991
ISBN 0-13-912544-2

For Piet

and all my friends in Texas

$\mathcal{M}$iss Mallard, the world-famous ducktective, was on vacation at a dude ranch in Texas. Late one afternoon she went horseback riding. Out on the trail, her horse was suddenly frightened by a bouncing tumbleweed and it reared up on its hind legs. Miss Mallard crashed to the ground, knitting bag and all. Then the horse galloped back to the ranch. Miss Mallard was left alone on the prairie to find her own way back.

Soon it grew dark. Miss Mallard saw some lights in the distance and headed toward them. At last she came to a huge, old house.

Miss Mallard firmly clutched her knitting bag and climbed the steps of the spooky-looking house. When she rang the doorbell, a housekeeper opened the door.

"I fell off my horse," said Miss Mallard. "And I am lost. May I use your telephone?"

The housekeeper invited her inside. There Miss Mallard met the owners of the house—Horace and Florence Butterball and their daughter, Cindy. With them were their guests, Phil and Tessie Scoter. They were all excited to have a famous ducktective in their midst.

"You *must* spend the night with us," said Florence Butterball, "and let us treat you to some Texas-style hospitality."

"Oh, but I can't," said Miss Mallard. "I'm expected back at the Duckaroo Dude Ranch. They are probably searching for me at this very moment."

"We'll call them!" said Horace Butterball. "You must stay for our cook-out tomorrow morning and then the celebration in our beautiful city of San Antonio. We're going to make a Texan out of you!"

"It does sound wonderful," said Miss Mallard. "But..."

"Good! Then it's settled!" said Florence Butterball.

She turned to the housekeeper.

"Mrs. Scaup," she said, "please call the ranch. Tell them that Miss Mallard is safe and that she will spend the night with us. Then prepare the Gold Room for her and tell Clarence, the cook, that we have another guest."

Mrs. Scaup said sourly, "I don't think Clarence will like the idea of an unexpected guest, Madam."

"Don't be silly," Florence Butterball replied. "He'll be thrilled when he learns that the guest is Miss Mallard, the famous ducktective."

Mrs. Scaup left in a huff.

Horace Butterball grumbled, "Our new housekeeper gives me the creeps."

"Now, now, dear," said his wife. "She's just being efficient. And she does manage the house well. She keeps it spotless. Haven't you noticed how she checks everything for dust with her white gloves?"

"Duck waddle!" said Horace. "Let's eat."

At dinner, the conversation was lively and interesting to Miss Mallard. Much of it was about Texas history, which she found fascinating. There was even an unsolved crime for her to ponder. Many old documents and treasures from Texas's history had recently been stolen from homes all over Texas. The only clues the police had were some telltale prints. But they could not identify the prints and find out who had stolen the documents and treasures.

"Here is *one* document the thieves will never get, Miss Mallard," said Horace Butterball after dinner. "We keep it in an old leather pouch that belonged to our first hero of early Texas, Sam Houston Drake."

Everyone gathered around a glass case in one corner of the dining room.

Horace Butterball opened the door of the glass case with a key. Then he took out the leather pouch. He opened the pouch and removed an old, torn parchment.

"This is one of the most treasured documents in all Texas," he said. "I am giving it to the State of Texas tomorrow at the Alamo National Monument in San Antonio. It is a list of the first 300 duck families who settled in Texas and it includes our family name."

"Phooey!" said Phil Scoter to his wife. "Our family name isn't on it. What's the big deal?"

"I hate that list!" snapped Tessie.

Horace was so eager to tell Miss Mallard about the list that he forgot how the Scoters felt about it. They were hurt and angry, and they acted as if they thought it was Horace's fault.

Horace didn't know how to make them feel better. Quickly, he returned the document to its pouch, placed the pouch back in the case, and locked the glass door.

"Well," he said, hoping to change the subject, "shall we all go to the library and look at some home movies?"

While the movies were being shown, the Scoters sat glum and silent. But they were not the only ones who felt angry. Cindy did too. That was because the movies were about *her*.

"Oh, Daddy, do you have to?" she protested every time another film began.

Finally, after the tenth movie about Cindy as a duckling, Florence Butterball said, "I think it's time for us to go to bed. The celebration breakfast will be at eight in the morning in the back yard. Then we must be at the Alamo by noon."

With that, everyone said goodnight.

Mrs. Scaup showed Miss Mallard to her room.

"Just pull the cord by the bed if you need anything," she said.

"Thank you," said Miss Mallard. She was about to set her knitting bag on a chair, but it toppled over and went tumbling to the floor. Mrs. Scaup stooped down to help pick up the things that spilled out.

"Do be careful," said Miss Mallard. "I have some sticky chocolates in there somewhere. I wouldn't want you to soil your gloves on them."

Mrs. Scaup quickly removed her gloves and picked up the chocolates, a small mirror, and some news items from Miss Mallard's clipping file. When everything was back in the bag, she put on her gloves and left.

Miss Mallard got ready for bed. She put on her nightgown and crawled under the covers. It had been a long, exhausting day for her. She fell sound asleep.

Later that night, she was awakened by a noise. She opened her eyes and saw a note being slipped under her door.

She ran to the door and opened it. She looked up and down the hall, but saw no one. She picked up the note and closed the door. By her bedside lamp she read:

DO NOT EAT THE BREAKFAST ROLLS.

FROM SOMEONE WHO CARES.

Miss Mallard shivered. What did the note mean?

Miss Mallard had trouble getting back to sleep. When at last she did, she was awakened again. Another note was being slipped under her door! This note said:

DO NOT DRINK THE JUICE AT BREAKFAST.

FROM SOMEONE WHO CARES.

Miss Mallard was wide awake after the second note. She tossed and turned in her bed the rest of the night. Finally, morning came. Feeling very worried, Miss Mallard went to breakfast.

Outside in the back yard, everyone was gathered around a table for the cook-out. Clarence, the cook, was flipping pancakes on an outdoor grill. Servants were heaping the table with great mounds of food. Mrs. Scaup stood close by to see that everything was done properly.

Horace Butterball was the first to see Miss Mallard.

"Come join us," he said. "Florence, pass the rolls. Cindy, pass the juice."

Miss Mallard sat down at the table. She watched a plate of breakfast rolls as it went around the table. One by one everyone took a roll. When the plate came to her, she quickly passed it on to the next person. She was the only one at the table who did not take a roll.

The same thing happened with the juice. She was the only one who did not fill her glass.

All through breakfast Miss Mallard picked at her pancakes. She watched the rolls being gobbled up and the juice being drunk by the others at the table. She felt very uneasy. She expected the worst.

All morning Miss Mallard waited. It was the longest meal of her life.

At last it was over. Miss Mallard heaved a sigh of relief. Nothing terrible had happened.

"Cindy," said Horace Butterball. "Please get the leather pouch from the glass case in the dining room. Here is the key. We'll have a toast to our ancestors to finish our feast. Then we'll be on our way to deliver the document to the State Museum at the Alamo."

Cindy went into the house, but she was back in a flash.

"Daddy!" she cried. "The leather pouch has been stolen!"

Everyone ran to the dining room and gathered around the glass case. They saw that the door to the case was broken. Sure enough, the leather pouch was gone!

"Step aside, everyone," said Miss Mallard. "Please don't touch anything."

"I'll call Sheriff Teal to come at once," said Horace Butterball.

"In the meantime, I'll check the glass case for prints," said Miss Mallard.

She took a magnifying glass from her knitting bag and examined the case. She saw many different prints. Then she remembered how everyone had gathered around the case after dinner. They must have left their prints on the glass then, she thought.

Sheriff Teal soon arrived. He examined the prints on the glass case. He compared them with a copy of some prints that he had brought with him.

"One thing is certain," he said. "None of the prints on this glass case match the ones from the other robberies. Whoever stole your leather pouch is not the robber we've been hunting for."

Everyone in the room looked at one another and gasped.

"You mean one of us could have stolen the pouch?" asked Florence Butterball.

"One—or all of you," said Sheriff Teal. "The prints tell the story. All of you have touched the case at one time or another. So it would be impossible to pin the robbery on any one of you. End of report."

He started to leave.

"Wait, Sheriff," said Miss Mallard. "May I have a copy of the prints you brought—the prints that belong to the crook who committed the other robberies?"

Sheriff Teal handed Miss Mallard a copy of the robber's prints. Then he turned to leave.

"But, Sheriff!" pleaded Horace Butterball. "How can you leave like this? A treasured document has been stolen. What can I tell the crowd at the Alamo?"

"That's up to you," said Sheriff Teal. "I have no case here. All I can do is file a report and hope something turns up. Goodbye."

As Sheriff Teal left, the Scoters announced that they were going home.

"You can't leave now!" Horace Butterball said to the Scoters. "You must help us find that document!"

"Phooey!" said Phil Scoter. "Who cares about that!"

A big argument started between the two. While they hollered at each other, Florence Butterball started quarreling with Clarence, the cook.

"After all," she shouted, "you were up all night preparing the breakfast. You should have been listening for robbers."

"I didn't know I was hired to cook for this place and guard it, too," snapped Clarence.

Meanwhile Tessie Scoter started a quarrel with Cindy and Mrs. Scaup yelled at one of the servants, who yelled back.

The quarreling got noisier and noisier. Finally, Miss Mallard stood on a chair and quacked as loudly as she could:

QUIET!

The room was suddenly silent.

"There!" said Miss Mallard. "If you will all stay quiet for a moment, I'll tell you what happened to the document. First, we must bring back the sheriff before he drives away. Clarence! Get Sheriff Teal!"

When Sheriff Teal returned, he asked, "What is this all about?"

Miss Mallard responded, "You left before I could reveal some important information to you. Then things got a bit out of hand."

"What information?" asked Sheriff Teal.

"The identity of the thief who stole the historical treasures, including the one in this house," said Miss Mallard.

She took the small mirror from her knitting bag. There were prints on it. She held the mirror next to the copy of the robber's prints that the sheriff had given her. They were the same!

"I got the prints when I dropped my knitting bag," said Miss Mallard coolly. "The prints on the mirror were made with chocolate. They belong to..."

Before Miss Mallard could finish, Mrs. Scaup started to run.

"Stop her!" shouted Miss Mallard.

As Sheriff Teal grabbed Mrs. Scaup, the leather pouch fell out of her pocket.

"You're under arrest!" said Sheriff Teal.

"I suspected her as soon as I saw her white gloves," said Miss Mallard. "She pretended to be a housekeeper so she could steal historical treasures and documents and sell them for a lot of money. She wore gloves so she wouldn't leave telltale prints at the scenes of her crimes. That's why her prints were not on the glass case with all the others. And that's how I knew that she had the pouch."

"We owe you a big thanks, Miss Mallard," said Horace Butterball. "But how will we get to the Alamo in time to present the document?"

"I'll lead the way with my siren," said Sheriff Teal. "You'll be there in a jiffy."

They raced after the sheriff's car all the way to the Alamo. Horace Butterball took his place on the platform in front of a huge crowd. While everything was being set up, Miss Mallard turned to Clarence, the cook.

"Why did you put the notes under my door last night?" asked Miss Mallard.

Clarence blushed and said, "I wanted everything to be perfect for your first Texas cook-out. The rolls I was baking last night didn't turn out right. And the oranges for the juice weren't as good as usual."

"I thought that was it," said Miss Mallard.

Just then Horace Butterball stood up and began reading the names of the first 300 Texas families.

Everyone cheered as each name was
read. Then Horace came to the "M's."

"WYATT MALLARD!" he shouted.

Everyone cheered louder than ever.

"Goodness!" said Miss Mallard. "That's
my ancestor. I guess that makes me a
Texan."

48